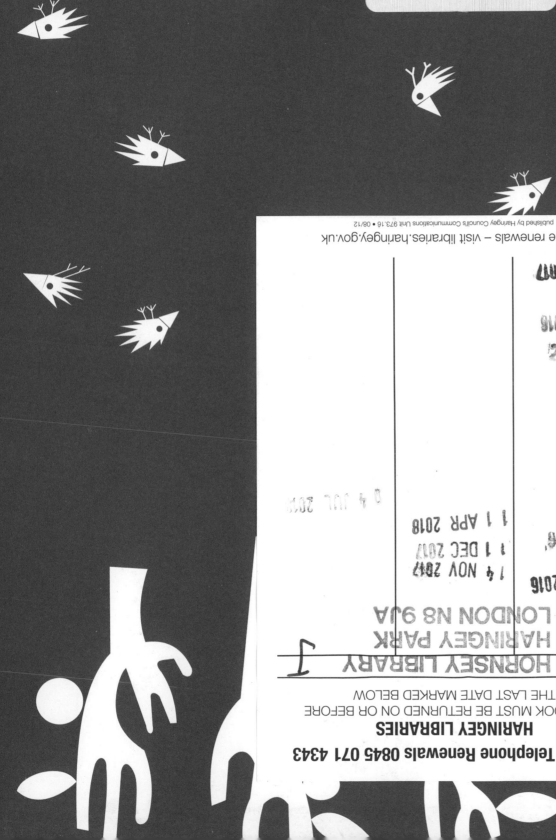

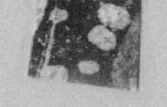

tiny owl publishing

© 2016 Tiny Owl Publishing Ltd
1 Repton House, Charlwood Street, SW1V 2LD, London, UK

Text and Illustration by Nahid Kazemi
Translated by Azita Rassi
Persian collection editor: Ali Seidabadi
Graphic designer: Elahe Javanmard

ISBN 978-1-910328-11-8

A catalogue record of this book is available from the British Library
www.tinyowl.co.uk

Tiny Owl Publishing Ltd,
Registered in England No. 08297587

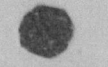

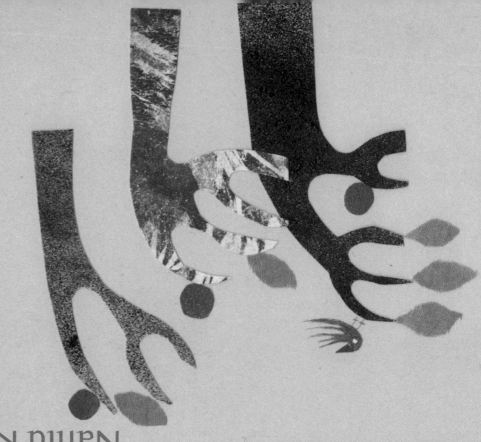

Nahid Kazemi

The Orange house

The Orange House lives at the end of an alley with tall buildings on both sides: the Sky Building, the Star Building, the Sea Building and the Moonlight Building.

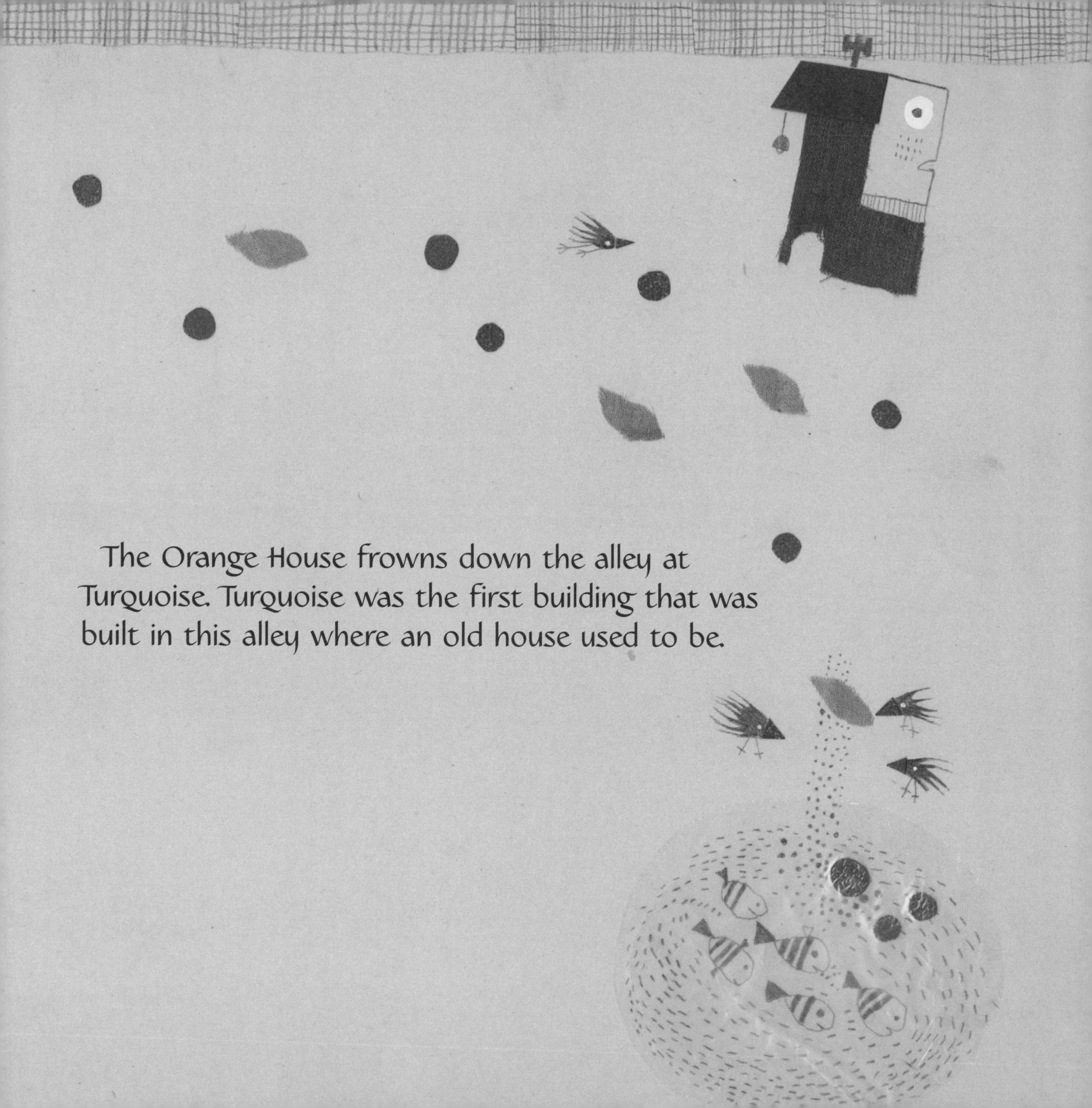

The Orange House frowns down the alley at Turquoise. Turquoise was the first building that was built in this alley where an old house used to be.

Nearby is a new building that doesn't have a name yet. Orange is the only old house left in the alley.

Sky, Star, Sea, Moonlight and Turquoise talk together. Each says something about the new building.

"What beautiful windows! The colour of the bricks is so pretty!" admires Sky.

"What staircases! What windows! The fences are so nice!" sighs Star.

"What a lift!" says Moonlight, dreamily.

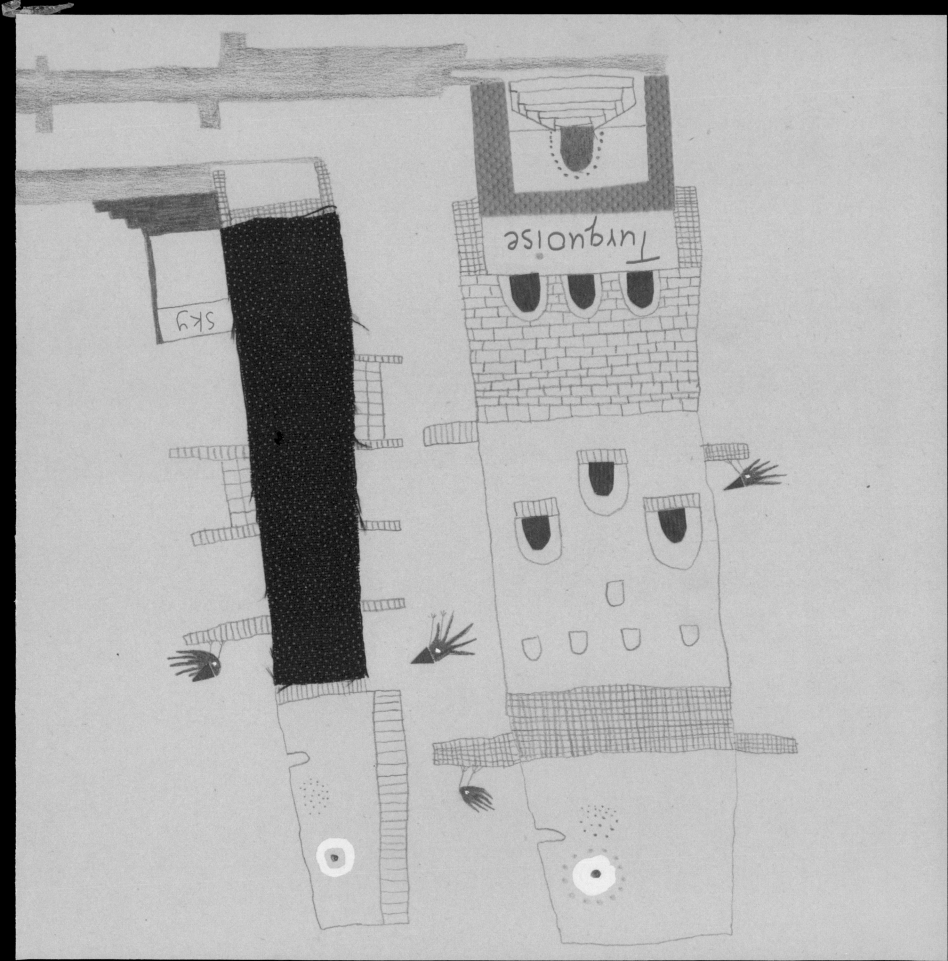

"Its plumbing is amazing. They say the pipes will never burst!" exclaims Sea, impressed.

The Orange House hears their words, but doesn't want to join in. She doesn't have a lift, only the old stone stairs. Her pipes have burst several times and then they have been fixed. She is a small, single-storey building.

Turquoise looks at the Orange House and asks, "What do you think? Don't you want to say something about our new friend?"

The Orange House doesn't speak.

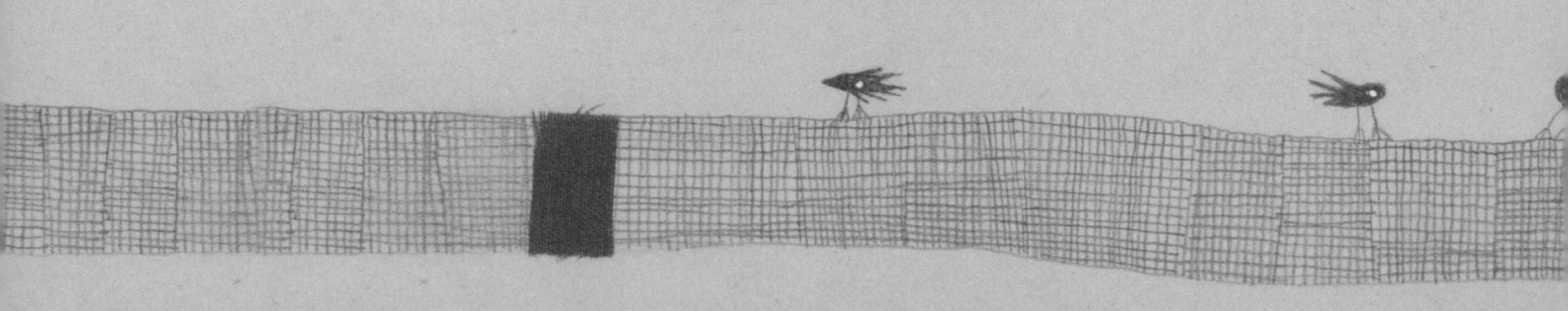

Turquoise

Sea

sky

Star

moonlight

"She never talks to us. She doesn't like us!" says
Moonlight, annoyed.

The Orange House remains quiet. "What have we done?
We've never hurt you," says Star.

The Orange House still refuses to speak.

Turquoise remembers something from years ago.
She says, "When I was built, none of you were here.

Instead there were some other houses in this alley, houses just like Orange. They had gardens full of trees, like Orange. They had ponds and fish and birds."

The Orange House becomes sadder after hearing this. She chokes on her tears.

Turquoise continues, "Every year, people tore one of those houses down and built us instead."

Moonlight looks at the Orange House and says, "Dear Orange! It's not our fault! We didn't know!"

"He's right," says Sea, kindly.

"We like you as well, Orange! We like your pretty garden, your orange trees, and your noisy crows!" says Sky.

"Yes and in those days the air was cleaner. It was easier to breathe. It wasn't like now," says Turquoise.

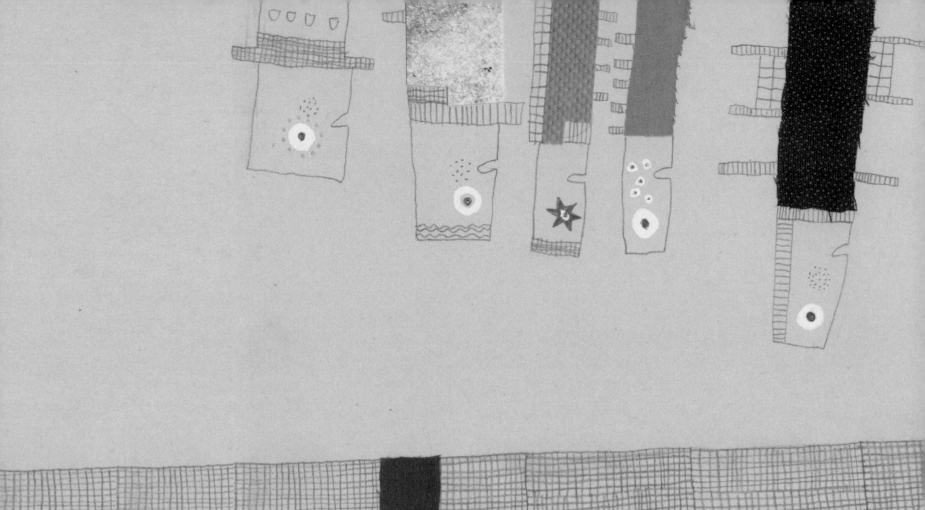
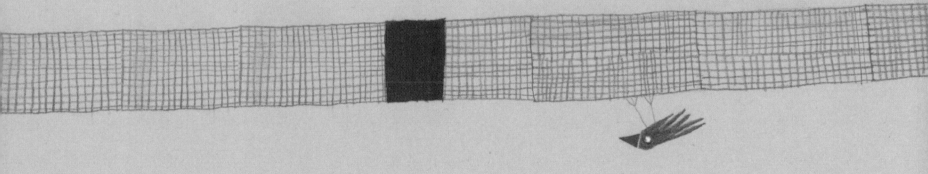
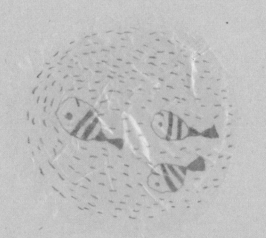

The Orange House looks up to say something.
Suddenly she sees people coming towards her from
the other end of the alley, holding shovels and
picks. She knows this can only mean one thing.
Turquoise peers to see what Orange is looking at.

She also sees them. The other buildings see them too.
  "We mustn't let them tear the Orange House down! The
Orange House keeps our alley more beautiful," says Sky.
  "Without her, we can't breathe easily," says Turquoise.

The tall buildings arrange themselves before the Orange House and block the way. The people with the shovels and picks walk up and down the alley, searching for the Orange House but they can't find her. They walk away without destroying her.

The Orange House smiles at the buildings of the alley for the first time. Old and new, they will live together and be friends.

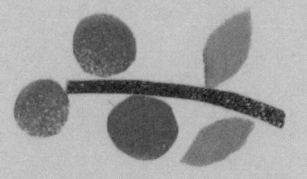

Nahid Kazemi

I started illustrating when I was a child, when I made books with my own hands and painted them. At that time I had the dream of making cheerful and colourful books instead of the boring ones.

When I grew up, I continued this path and studied art in university.

I received my masters in painting from Tehran Art University and started attending inland and outland festivals and have cooperated with publishers inside and outside my country, Iran. I have illustrated more than 50 books for children. I currently live in Canada.

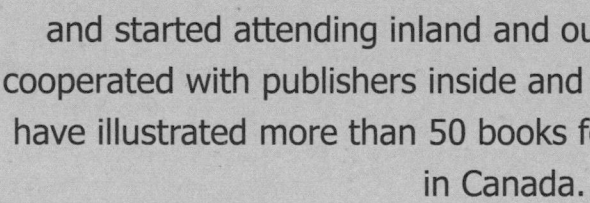

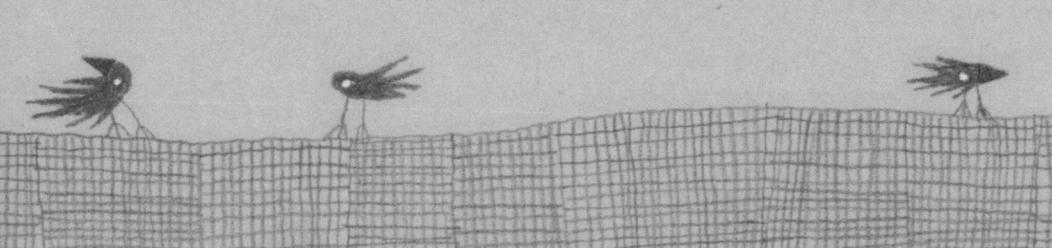